A Brush with the Chinese and What Came of it

Start Publishing PD LLC

Manufactured in the United States of America

Cover art: Shutterstock/Taisiya Kozorez

Cover design: Jennifer Do

10 9 8 7 6 5 4 3 2 1

ISBN 979-8-8809-0009-1

A Brush with the Chinese and What Came of it

G. A. Henty

It was early in December that H.M.S. Perseus was cruising off the mouth of the Canton River. War had been declared with China in consequence of her continued evasions of the treaty she had made with us, and it was expected that a strong naval force would soon gather to bring her to reason. In the meantime the ships on the station had a busy time of it, chasing the enemy's junks when they ventured to show themselves beyond the reach of the guns of their forts, and occasionally having a brush with the piratical boats which took advantage of the general confusion to plunder friend as well as foe.

The Perseus had that afternoon chased two Government junks up a creek. The sun had already set when they took refuge there, and the captain did not care to send his boats after them in the dark, as many of the creeks ran up for miles into the flat country; and as they not unfrequently had many arms or branches, the boats might, in the dark, miss the junks altogether. Orders were issued that four boats should be ready for starting at daybreak the next morning. The Perseus anchored off the mouth of the creek, and two boats were ordered to row backwards and forwards off its mouth all night to insure that the enemy did not slip out in the darkness.

Jack Fothergill, the senior midshipman, was commanding the gig, and two of the other midshipmen were going in the pinnace and launch, commanded respectively by the first lieutenant and the master. The three other midshipmen of the Perseus were loud in their lamentations that they were not to take share in the fun.

"You can't all go, you know," Fothergill said, "and it's no use making a row about it; the captain has been very good to let three of us go."

"It's all very well for you, Jack," Percy Adcock, the youngest of the lads, replied, "because you are one of those chosen; and it is not so hard for Simmons and Linthorpe, because they went the other day in the boat that chased those junks under shelter of the guns of their battery, but I haven't had a chance for ever so long."

"What fun was there in chasing the junks?" Simmons said. "We never got near the brutes till they were close to their battery, and then just as the first shot came singing from their guns, and we thought that we were going to have some excitement, the first lieutenant sung out 'Easy all,' and there was nothing for it but to turn round and to row for the ship, and a nice hot row it was—two hours and a half in a broiling sun. Of course I am not blaming Oliphant, for the captain's orders were strict that we were not to try to cut the junks out if they got under the guns of any of their batteries.

Still it was horribly annoying, and I do think the captain might have remembered what beastly luck we had last time, and given us a chance to-morrow."

"It is clear we could not all go," Fothergill said, "and naturally enough the captain chose the three seniors. Besides, if you did have bad luck last time, you had your chance, and I don't suppose we shall have anything more exciting now; these fellows always set fire to their junks and row for the shore directly they see us, after firing a shot or two wildly in our direction."

"Well, Jack, if you don't expect any fun," Simmons replied, "perhaps you wouldn't mind telling the first lieutenant you do not care for going, and that I am very anxious to take your place. Perhaps he will be good enough to allow me to relieve you."

"A likely thing that!" Fothergill laughed. "No, Tom, I am sorry you are not going, but you must make the best of it till another chance comes."

"Don't you think, Jack," Percy Adcock said to his senior in a coaxing tone later on, "you could manage to smuggle me into the boat with you?"

"Not I, Percy. Suppose you got hurt, what would the captain say then? And firing as wildly as the Chinese do, a shot is just as likely to hit your little carcase as to lodge in one of the sailors. No, you must just make the best of it, Percy, and I promise you that next time there is a boat expedition, if you are not put in, I will say a good word to the first luff for you."

"That promise is better than nothing," the boy said; "but I would a deal rather go this time and take my chance next."

"But you see you can't, Percy, and there's no use talking any more about it. I really do not expect there will be any fighting. Two junks would hardly make any opposition to the boats of the ship, and I expect we shall be back by nine o'clock with the news that they were well on fire before we came up."

Percy Adcock, however, was determined, if possible, to go. He was a favourite among the men, and when he spoke to the bow oar of the gig, the latter promised to do anything he could to aid him to carry out his wishes.

"We are to start at daybreak, Tom, so that it will be quite dark when the boats are lowered. I will creep into the gig before that and hide myself as well as I can under your thwart, and all you have got to do is to take no notice of me. When the boat is lowered I think they will hardly make me out from the deck, especially as you will be standing up in the bow holding on with the boat-hook till the rest get on board."

"Well, sir, I will do my best; but if you are caught you must not let out that I knew anything about it."

"I won't do that," Percy said. "I don't think there is much chance of my being noticed until we get on board the junks, and then they won't know which boat I came off in, and the first lieutenant will be too busy to blow me up. Of course I shall get it when I am on board again, but I don't mind that so that I see the fun. Besides, I want to send home some things to my sister, and she will like them all the better if I can tell her I captured them on board some junks we seized and burnt."

The next morning the crews mustered before daybreak. Percy had already taken his place under the bow thwart of the gig. The davits were swung overboard, and two men took their places in her as she was lowered down by the falls. As soon as she touched the water the rest of the crew clambered down by the ladder and took their places; then Fothergill took his seat in the stern, and the boat pushed off and lay a few lengths away from the ship until the heavier boats put off. As soon as they were under way Percy crawled out from his hiding-place and placed himself in the bow, where he was sheltered by the body of the oarsmen from Fothergill's sight.

Day was just breaking now, but it was still dark on the water, and the boat rowed very slowly until it became lighter. Percy could just make out the shores of the creek on both sides; they were but two or three feet above the level of the water, and were evidently submerged at high tide. The creek was about a hundred yards wide, and the lad could not see far ahead, for it was full of sharp windings and turnings. Here and there branches joined it, but the boats were evidently following the main channel. After another half-hour's rowing the first lieutenant suddenly gave the order, "Easy all," and the men, looking over their shoulders, saw a village a quarter of a mile ahead, with the two junks they had chased the night before lying in front of it. Almost at the same moment a sudden uproar was heard—drums were beaten and gongs sounded.

"They are on the look-out for us," the first lieutenant said. "Mr. Mason, do you keep with me and attack the junk highest up the river; Mr. Bellew and Mr. Fothergill, do you take the one lower down. Row on, men."

The oars all touched the water together, and the four boats leapt forward. In a minute a scattering fire of gingals and matchlocks was opened from the junks, and the bullets pattered on the water round the boats. Percy was kneeling up in the bow now. As they passed a branch channel three or four hundred yards from the village, he started and leapt to his feet.

"There are four or five junks in that passage, Fothergill; they are poling out."

The first lieutenant heard the words.

"Row on, men; let us finish with these craft ahead before the others get out. This must be that piratical village we have heard about, Mr. Mason, as lying up one of these creeks; that accounts for those two junks not going higher up. I was surprised at seeing them here, for they might guess that we should try to get them this morning. Evidently they calculated on catching us in a trap."

Percy was delighted at finding that, in the excitement caused by his news, the first lieutenant had forgotten to take any notice of his being there without orders, and he returned a defiant nod to the threat conveyed by Fothergill shaking his fist at him. As they neared the junks the fire of those on board redoubled, and was aided by that of many villagers gathered on the bank of the creek. Suddenly from a bank of rushes four cannons were fired. A ball struck the pinnace, smashing in her side. The other boats gathered hastily round and took her crew on board, and then dashed at the junks, which were but a hundred yards distant. The valour of the Chinese evaporated as they saw the boats approaching, and scores of them leapt overboard and swam for shore.

In another minute the boats were alongside and the crews scrambling up the sides of the junks. A few Chinamen only attempted to oppose them. These were speedily overcome, and the British had now time to look round, and saw that six junks crowded with men had issued from the side creek and were making towards them.

"Let the boats tow astern," the lieutenant ordered. "We should have to run the gauntlet of that battery on shore if we were to attack them, and might lose another boat before we reached their side. We will fight them here."

The junks approached, those on board firing their guns, yelling and shouting, while the drums and gongs were furiously beaten.

"They will find themselves mistaken, Percy, if they think they are going to frighten us with all that row," Fothergill said. "You young rascal, how did you get on board the boat without being seen? The captain will be sure to suspect I had a hand in concealing you."

The tars were now at work firing the gingals attached to the bulwarks and the matchlocks, with which the deck was strewn, at the approaching junks. As they took steady aim, leaning their pieces on the bulwarks, they did considerable execution among the Chinamen crowded on board the junks, while the shot of the Chinese, for the most part, whistled far overhead; but the guns of the shore battery, which had now been slewed round to bear upon them, opened with a better aim, and several shots came crashing into the sides of the two captured junks.

"Get ready to board, lads!" Lieutenant Oliphant shouted. "Don't wait for them to board you, but the moment they come alongside lash their rigging to ours and spring on board them."

The leading junk was now about twenty yards away, and presently grated alongside. Half-a-dozen sailors at once sprang into her rigging with ropes, and after lashing the junks together leaped down upon her deck, where Fothergill was leading the gig's crew and some of those rescued from the pinnace, while Mr. Bellew, with another party, had boarded her at the stern. Several of the Chinese fought stoutly, but the greater part lost heart at seeing themselves attacked by the "white devils," instead of, as they expected, overwhelming them by their superior numbers. Many began at once to jump overboard, and after two or three minutes' sharp fighting, the rest either followed their example or were beaten below.

Fothergill looked round. The other junk had been attacked by two of the enemy, one on each side, and the little body of sailors were gathered in her waist, and were defending themselves against an overwhelming number of the enemy.

The other three piratical junks had been carried somewhat up the creek by the tide that was sweeping inward, and could not for the moment take part in the fight.

"Mr. Oliphant is hard pressed, sir." He asked the master: "Shall we take to the boats?"

"That will be the best plan," Mr. Bellew replied. "Quick, lads, get the boats alongside and tumble in; there is not a moment to be lost."

The crew at once sprang to the boats and rowed to the other junk, which was but some thirty yards away.

The Chinese, absorbed in their contest with the crew of the pinnace, did not perceive the new-comers until they gained the deck, and with a shout fell furiously upon them. In their surprise and consternation the pirates did not pause to note that they were still five to one superior in number, but made a precipitate rush for their own vessels. The English at once took the offensive. The first lieutenant with his party boarded one, while the new-comers leapt on to the deck of the other. The panic which had seized the Chinese was so complete that they attempted no resistance whatever, but sprang overboard in great numbers and swam to the shore, which was but twenty yards away, and in three minutes the English were in undisputed possession of both vessels.

"Back again, Mr. Fothergill, or you will lose the craft you captured," Lieutenant Oliphant said; "they have already cut her free."

The Chinese, indeed, who had been beaten below by the boarding party, had soon perceived the sudden departure of their captors, and gaining the deck again had cut the lashings which fastened them to the other junk, and were proceeding to hoist their sails. They were too late, however. Almost before the craft had way on her Fothergill and his crew were alongside. The Chinese did not wait for the attack, but at once sprang overboard and made for the shore. The other three junks, seeing the capture of their comrades, had already hoisted their sails and were making up the creek. Fothergill dropped an anchor, left four of his men in charge, and rowed back to Mr. Oliphant.

"What shall we do next, sir?"

"We will give those fellows on shore a lesson, and silence their battery. Two men have been killed since you left. We must let the other junks go for the present. Four of my men were killed and eleven wounded before Mr. Bellew and you came to our assistance. The Chinese were fighting pluckily up to that time, and it would have gone very hard with us if you had not been at hand; the beggars will fight when they think they have got it all their own way. But before we land we will set fire to the five junks we have taken. Do you return and see that the two astern are well lighted, Mr. Fothergill; Mr. Mason will see to these three. When you have done your work take to your boat and lay off till I join you; keep the junks between you and the shore, to protect you from the fire of the rascals there."

"I cannot come with you, I suppose, Fothergill?" Percy Adcock said, as the midshipman was about to descend into his boat again.

"Yes, come along, Percy. It doesn't matter what you do now. The captain will be so pleased when he hears that we have captured and burnt five junks, that you will get off with a very light wigging, I imagine."

"That's just what I was thinking, Jack. Has it not been fun?"

"You wouldn't have thought it fun if you had got one of those matchlock balls in your body. There are a good many of our poor fellows just at the present moment who do not see anything funny in the affair at all. Here we are; clamber up."

The crew soon set to work under Fothergill's orders. The sails were cut off the masts and thrown down into the hold; bamboos, of which there were an abundance down there, were heaped over them, a barrel of oil was poured over the mass, and the fire then applied.

"That will do, lads. Now take to your boats and let's make a bonfire of the other junk."

In ten minutes both vessels were a sheet of flame, and the boat was lying a short distance from them waiting for further operations. The inhabitants of the village, furious at the failure of the plan which had been laid for the destruction of the "white devils," kept up a constant fusilade, which, however, did no harm, for the gig was completely sheltered by the burning junks close to her from their missiles.

"There go the others!" Percy exclaimed after a minute or two, as three columns of smoke arose simultaneously from the other junks, and the sailors were seen dropping into their boats alongside.

The killed and wounded were placed in the other gig with four sailors in charge. They were directed to keep under shelter of the junks until rejoined by the pinnace and Fothergill's gig, after these had done their work on shore.

When all was ready the first lieutenant raised his hand as a signal, and the two boats dashed between the burning junks and rowed for the shore. Such of the natives as had their weapons charged fired a hasty volley, and then, as the sailors leapt from their boats, took to their heels.

"Mr. Fothergill, take your party into the village and set fire to the houses; shoot down every man you see. This place is a nest of pirates. I will capture that battery and then join you."

Fothergill and his sailors at once entered the village. The men had already fled; the women were turned out of the houses, and these were immediately set on fire. The tars regarded the whole affair as a glorious joke, and raced from house to house, making a hasty search in each for concealed valuables before setting it on fire. In a short time the whole village was in a blaze.

"There is a house there, standing in that little grove a hundred yards away," Percy said.

"It looks like a temple," Fothergill replied. "However, we will have a look at it." And calling two sailors to accompany him, he started at a run towards it, Percy keeping by his side.

"It is a temple," Fothergill said when they approached it. "Still, we will have a look at it, but we won't burn it; it will be as well to respect the religion, even of a set of piratical scoundrels like these."

At the head of his men he rushed in at the entrance. There was a blaze of fire as half a dozen muskets were discharged in their faces. One of the sailors dropped dead, and before the others had time to realize what had happened they were beaten to the ground by a storm of blows from swords and other weapons.

A heavy blow crashed down on Percy's head, and he fell insensible even before he realized what had occurred.

When he recovered, his first sensation was that of a vague wonder as to what had happened to him. He seemed to be in darkness and unable to move hand or foot. He was compressed in some way that he could not at first understand, and was being bumped and jolted in an extraordinary manner. It was some little time before he could understand the situation. He first remembered the fight with the junks, then he recalled the landing and burning the village; then, as his brain cleared, came the recollection of his start with Fothergill for the temple among the trees, his arrival there, and a loud report and flash of fire.

"I must have been knocked down and stunned," he said to himself, "and I suppose I am a prisoner now to these brutes, and one of them must be carrying me on his back."

Yes, he could understand it all now. His hands and his feet were tied, ropes were passed round his body in every direction, and he was fastened back to back upon the shoulders of a Chinaman. Percy remembered the tales he had heard of the imprisonment and torture of those who fell into the hands of the Chinese, and he bitterly regretted that he had not been killed instead of stunned in the surprise of the temple.

"It would have been just the same feeling," he said to himself, "and there would have been an end of it. Now, there is no saying what is going to happen. I wonder whether Jack was killed, and the sailors."

Presently there was a jabber of voices; the motion ceased. Percy could feel that the cords were being unwound, and he was dropped on to his feet; then the cloth was removed from his head, and he could look round.

A dozen Chinese, armed with matchlocks and bristling with swords and daggers, stood around, and among them, bound like himself and gagged by a piece of bamboo forced lengthways across his mouth and kept there with a string going round the back of the head, stood Fothergill. He was bleeding from several cuts in the head. Percy's heart gave a bound of joy at finding that he was not alone; then he tried to feel sorry that Jack had not escaped, but failed to do so, although he told himself that his comrade's presence would not in any way alleviate the fate which was certain to befall him.

Still the thought of companionship, even in wretchedness, and perhaps a vague hope that Jack, with his energy and spirit, might contrive some way for their escape, cheered him up.

As Percy, too, was gagged, no word could be exchanged by the midshipmen, but they nodded to each other. They were now put side by side and made to walk in the centre of their captors. On the way they passed through several villages, whose inhabitants poured out to gaze at the captives, but the men in charge of them were evidently not disposed to delay, as they passed through without a stop. At last they halted before two cottages standing by themselves, thrust the prisoners into a small room, removed their gags, and left them to themselves.

"Well, Percy, my boy, so they caught you too? I am awfully sorry. It was my fault for going with only two men into that temple, but as the village had been deserted and scarcely a man was found there, it never entered my mind that there might be a party in the temple."

"Of course not, Jack; it was a surprise altogether. I don't know anything about it, for I was knocked down, I suppose, just as we went in, and the first thing I knew about it was that I was being carried on the back of one of those fellows. I thought it was awful at first, but I don't seem to mind so much now you are with me."

"It is a comfort to have someone to speak to," Jack said, "yet I wish you were not here, Percy; I can't do you any good, and I shall never cease blaming myself for having brought you into this scrape. I don't know much more about the affair than you do. The guns were fired so close to us that my face was scorched with one of them, and almost at the same instant I got a lick across my cheek with a sword. I had just time to hit at one of them, and then almost at the same moment I got two or three other blows, and down I went; they threw themselves on the top of me and tied and gagged me in no time. Then I was tied to a long bamboo, and two fellows put the ends on their shoulders and went off with me through the fields. Of course I was face downwards, and did not know you were with us till they stopped and loosed me from the bamboo and set me on my feet."

"But what are they going to do with us do you think, Jack?"

"I should say they are going to take us to Canton and claim a reward for our capture, and there I suppose they will cut off our heads or saw us in two, or put us to some other unpleasant kind of death. I expect they are discussing it now; do you hear what a jabber they are kicking up?"

Voices were indeed heard raised in angry altercation in the next room. After a time the din subsided and the conversation appeared to take a more amiable turn.

"I suppose they have settled it as far as they are concerned," Jack said; "anyhow, you may be quite sure they mean to make something out of us. If they hadn't they would have finished us at once, for they must have been furious at the destruction of their junks and village. As to the idea that mercy has anything to do with it, we may as well put it out of our minds. The Chinaman, at the best of times, has no feeling of pity in his nature, and after their defeat it is certain they would have killed us at once had they not hoped to do better by us. If they had been Indians I should have said they had carried us off to enjoy the satisfaction of torturing us, but I don't suppose it is that with them."

"Do you think there is any chance of our getting away?" Percy asked, after a pause.

"I should say not the least in the world, Percy. My hands are fastened so tight now that the ropes seem cutting into my wrists, and after they had set me on my feet and cut the cords of my legs I could scarcely stand at first, my feet were so numbed by the pressure. However, we must keep up our pluck. Possibly they may keep us at Canton for a bit, and if they do the squadron may arrive and fight its way past the forts and take the city before they have quite made up their minds as to what kind of death will be most appropriate to the occasion. I wonder what they are doing now? They seem to be chopping sticks."

"I wish they would give us some water," Percy said. "I am frightfully thirsty."

"And so am I, Percy; there is one comfort, they won't let us die of thirst, they could get no satisfaction out of our deaths now."

Two hours later some of the Chinese re-entered the room and led the captives outside, and the lads then saw what was the meaning of the noise they had heard. A cage had been manufactured of strong bamboos. It was about four and a half feet long, four feet wide, and less than three feet high; above it was fastened two long bamboos. Two or three of the bars of the cage had been left open.

"My goodness! they never intend to put us in there," Percy exclaimed.

"That they do," Jack said. "They are going to carry us the rest of the way."

The cords which bound the prisoners' hands were now cut, and they were motioned to crawl into the cage. This they did; the bars were then put in their places and securely lashed. Four men went to the ends of the poles and lifted the cage upon their shoulders; two others took their places beside it, and one man, apparently the leader of the party, walked on ahead; the rest remained behind.

"I never quite realized what a fowl felt in a coop before," Jack said, "but if its sensations are at all like mine they must be decidedly unpleasant. It isn't high enough to sit upright in, it is nothing like long enough to lie down, and as to getting out one might as well think of flying. Do you know, Percy, I don't think they mean taking us to Canton at all. I did not think of it before, but from the direction of the sun I feel sure that we cannot have been going that way. What they are up to I can't imagine."

In an hour they came to a large village. Here the cage was set down and the villagers closed round. They were, however, kept a short distance from the cage by the men in charge of it. Then a wooden platter was placed on the ground, and persons throwing a few copper coins into this were allowed to come near the cage.

"They are making a show of us!" Fothergill exclaimed. "That's what they are up to, you see if it isn't; they are going to travel up country to show the 'white devils' whom their valour has captured."

This was, indeed, the purpose of the pirates. At that time Europeans seldom ventured beyond the limits assigned to them in the two or three towns where they were permitted to trade, and few, indeed, of the country people had ever obtained a sight of the white barbarians of whose doings they had so frequently heard. Consequently a small crowd soon gathered round the cage, eyeing the captives with the same interest they would have felt as to unknown and dangerous beasts; they laughed and joked, passed remarks upon them, and even poked them with sticks. Fothergill, furious at this treatment, caught one of the sticks, and wrenching it from the hands of the Chinaman, tried to strike at him through the bars, a proceeding which excited shouts of laughter from the by-standers.

"I think, Jack," Percy said, "it will be best to try and keep our tempers and not to seem to mind what they do to us, then if they find they can't get any fun out of us they will soon leave us alone."

"Of course, that's the best plan," Fothergill agreed, "but it's not so easy to follow. That fellow very nearly poked out my eye with his stick, and no one's going to stand that if he can help it."

It was some hours before the curiosity of the village was satisfied. When all had paid who were likely to do so, the guards broke up their circle, and leaving two of their number at the cage to see that no actual harm was caused to their prisoners, the rest went off to a refreshment house. The place of the elders was now taken by the boys and children of the village, who crowded round the cage, prodded the prisoners with sticks, and, putting their hands through the bars, pulled their ears and hair. This amusement, however, was brought to an abrupt conclusion by Fothergill suddenly seizing the wrist of a big boy and pulling his arm through the cage until his face was against the bars; then he proceeded to punch him until the guard, coming to his rescue, poked Fothergill with his stick until he released his hold.

The punishment of their comrade excited neither anger nor resentment among the other boys, who yelled with delight at his discomfiture, but it made them more careful in approaching the cage, and though they continued to poke the prisoners with sticks they did not venture again to thrust a hand through the bars. At sunset the guards again came round, lifted the cage and carried it into a shed. A platter of dirty rice and a jug of water were put into the cage; two of the men lighted their long pipes and sat down on guard beside it, and, the doors being closed, the captives were left in peace.

"If this sort of thing is to go on, as I suppose it is," Fothergill said, "the sooner they cut off our heads the better."

"It is very bad, Jack. I am sore all over with those probes from their sharp sticks."

"I don't care for the pain, Percy, so much as the humiliation of the thing. To be stared at and poked at as if we were wild beasts by these curs, when with half a dozen of our men we could send a hundred of them scampering, I feel as if I could choke with rage."

"You had better try and eat some of this rice, Jack. It is beastly, but I daresay we shall get no more until to-morrow night, and we must keep up our strength if we can. At any rate, the water is not bad, that's a comfort."

"No thanks to them," Jack growled. "If there had been any bad water in the neighbourhood they would have given it to us."

For six weeks the sufferings of the prisoners continued. Their captors avoided towns where the authorities would probably at once have taken the prisoners out of their hands. No one would have recognized the two captives as the midshipmen of the Perseus; their clothes were in rags—torn to pieces by the thrusts of the sharp-pointed bamboos, to which they had daily been subjected—the bad food, the cramped position, and the misery which they suffered had worn both lads to skeletons; their hair was matted with filth, their faces begrimed with dirt. Percy was so weak that he felt he could not stand. Fothergill, being three years older, was less exhausted, but he knew that he, too, could not support his sufferings for many days longer. Their bodies were covered with sores, and try as they would they were able to catch only a few minutes' sleep at a time, so much did the bamboo bars hurt their wasted limbs.

They seldom exchanged a word during the daytime, suffering in silence the persecutions to which they were exposed, but at night they talked over their homes and friends in England, and their comrades on board ship, seldom saying a word as to their present position. They were now in a hilly country, but had not the least idea of the direction in which it lay from Canton or its distance from the coast.

One evening Jack said to his companion, "I think it's nearly all over now, Percy. The last two days we have made longer journeys, and have not stopped at any of the smaller villages we passed through. I fancy our guards must see that we can't last much longer, and are taking us down to some town to hand us over to the authorities and get their reward for us."

"I hope it is so, Jack; the sooner the better. Not that it makes much difference now to me, for I do not think I can stand many more days of it."

"I am afraid I am tougher than you, Percy, and shall take longer to kill, so I hope with all my heart that I may be right, and that they may be going to give us up to the authorities."

The next evening they stopped at a large place, and were subjected to the usual persecution; this, however, was now less prolonged than during the early days of their captivity, for they had now no longer strength or spirits to resent their treatment, and as no fun was to be obtained from passive victims, even the village boys soon ceased to find any amusement in tormenting them.

When most of their visitors had left them, an elderly Chinaman approached the side of the cage. He spoke to their guards and looked at them attentively for some minutes, then he said in pigeon English, "You officer men?"

"Yes!" Jack exclaimed, starting at the sound of the English words, the first they had heard spoken since their captivity. "Yes, we are officers of the Perseus."

"Me speeke English velly well," the Chinaman said; "me pilot-man many years on Canton river. How you get here?"

"We were attacking some piratical junks, and landed to destroy the village where the people were firing on us. We entered a place full of pirates, and were knocked down and taken prisoners, and carried away up the country; that is six weeks ago, and you see what we are now."

"Pirate men velly bad," the Chinaman said; "plunder many junk on river and kill crew. Me muchee hate them."

"Can you do anything for us?" Jack asked. "You will be well rewarded if you could manage to get us free."

The man shook his head.

"Me no see what can do, me stranger here; come to stay with wifey; people no do what me ask them. English ships attack Canton, much fight and take town, people all hate English. Bad country dis. People in one village fight against another. Velly bad men here."

"How far is Canton away?" Jack asked. "Could you not send down to tell the English we are here?"

"Fourteen days' journey off," the man said; "no see how can do anything."

"Well," Jack said, "when you get back again to Canton let our people know what has been the end of us; we shall not last much longer."

"All light," the man said, "will see what me can do. Muchee think to-night!" And after saying a few words to the guards, who had been regarding this conversation with an air of surprise, the Chinaman retired.

The guards had for some time abandoned the precaution of sitting up at night by the cage, convinced that their captives had no longer strength to attempt to break through its fastenings or to drag themselves many yards away if they could do so. They therefore left it standing in the open, and, wrapping themselves in their thickly-wadded coats, for the nights were cold, lay down by the side of the cage.

The coolness of the nights had, indeed, assisted to keep the two prisoners alive. During the day the sun was excessively hot, and the crowd of visitors round the cage impeded the circulation of the air and added to their sufferings. It was true that the cold at night frequently prevented them from sleeping, but it acted as a tonic and braced them up.

"What did he mean about the villages attacking each other?" Percy asked.

"I have heard," Jack replied, "that in some parts of China things are very much the same as they used to be in the highlands of Scotland. There is no law or order. The different villages are like clans, and wage war on each other. Sometimes the Government sends a number of troops, who put the thing down for a time, chop off a good many heads, and then march away, and the whole work begins again as soon as their backs are turned."

That night the uneasy slumber of the lads was disturbed by a sudden firing; shouts and yells were heard, and the firing redoubled.

"The village is attacked," Jack said. "I noticed that, like some other places we have come into lately, there is a strong earthen wall round it, with gates. Well, there is one comfort—it does not make much difference to us which side wins."

The guards at the first alarm leapt to their feet, caught up their matchlocks, and ran to aid in the defence of the wall. Two minutes later a man ran up to the cage.

"All lightee," he said; "just what me hopee."

With his knife he cut the tough withes that held the bamboos in their places, and pulled out three of the bars.

"Come along," he said; "no time to lose."

Jack scrambled out, but in trying to stand upright gave a sharp exclamation of pain. Percy crawled out more slowly; he tried to stand up, but could not. The Chinaman caught him up and threw him on his shoulder.

"Come along quickee," he said to Jack; "if takee village, kill evely one." He set off at a run. Jack followed as fast as he could, groaning at every step from the pain the movement caused to his bruised body.

They went to the side of the village opposite to that at which the attack was going on. They met no one on the way, the inhabitants having all rushed to the other side to repel the attack. They stopped at a small gate in the wall, the Chinaman drew back the bolts and opened it, and they passed out into the country. For an hour they kept on. By the end of that time Jack could scarcely drag his limbs along. The Chinaman halted at length in a clump of trees surrounded by a thick undergrowth.

"Allee safee here," he said, "no searchee so far; here food;" and he produced from a wallet a cold chicken and some boiled rice, and unslung from his shoulder a gourd filled with cold tea.

"Me go back now, see what happen. To-mollow nightee come again—bringee more food." And without another word went off at a rapid pace.

Jack moistened his lips with the tea, and then turned to his companion. Percy had not spoken a word since he had been released from the cage, and had been insensible during the greater part of his journey. Jack poured some cold tea between his lips.

"Cheer up, Percy, old boy, we are free now, and with luck and that good fellow's help we will work our way down to Canton yet."

"I shall never get down there; you may," Percy said feebly.

"Oh, nonsense, you will pick up strength like a steam-engine now. Here, let me prop you against this tree. That's better. Now drink a drop of this tea; it's like nectar after that filthy water we have been drinking. Now you will feel better. Now you must try and eat a little of this chicken and rice. Oh, nonsense, you have got to do it. I am not going to let you give way when our trouble is just over. Think of your people at home, Percy, and make an effort, for their sakes. Good heavens! now I think of it, it must be Christmas morning. We were caught on the 2nd and we have been just twenty-two days on show. I am sure that it must be past twelve o'clock, and it is Christmas-day. It is a good omen, Percy. This food isn't like roast beef and plum-pudding, but it's not to be despised, I can tell you. Come, fire away, that's a good fellow."

Percy made an effort and ate a few mouthfuls of rice and chicken, then he took another draught of tea, and lay down, and was almost immediately asleep.

Jack ate his food slowly and contentedly till he finished half the supply, then he, too, lay down, and, after a short but hearty thanksgiving for his escape from a slow and lingering death, he, too, fell off to sleep. The sun was rising when he woke, being aroused by a slight movement on the part of Percy; he opened his eyes and sat up.

"Well, Percy, how do you feel this morning?" he asked cheerily.

"I feel too weak to move," Percy replied languidly.

"Oh, you will be all right when you have sat up and eaten breakfast," Jack said. "Here you are; here is a wing for you, and this rice is as white as snow, and the tea is first rate. I thought last night after I lay down that I heard a murmur of water, so after we have had breakfast I will look about and see if I can find it. We should feel like new men after a wash. You look awful, and I am sure I am just as bad."

The thought of a wash inspirited Percy far more than that of eating, and he sat up and made a great effort to do justice to breakfast. He succeeded much better than he had done the night before, and Jack, although he pretended to grumble, was satisfied with his companion's progress, and finished off the rest of the food. Then he set out to search for water. He had not very far to go; a tiny stream, a few inches wide and two or three inches deep, ran through the wood from the higher ground. After throwing himself down and taking a drink, he hurried back to Percy.

"It is all right, Percy, I have found it. We can wash to our hearts' content; think of that, lad."

Percy could hardly stand, but he made an effort, and Jack half carried him to the streamlet. There the lads spent hours. First they bathed their heads and hands, and then, stripping, lay down in the stream and allowed it to flow over them, then they rubbed themselves with handfuls of leaves dipped in the water, and when they at last put on their rags again felt like new men. Percy was able to walk back to the spot they had quitted with the assistance only of Jack's arm. The latter, feeling that his breakfast had by no means appeased his hunger, now started for a search through the wood, and presently returned to Percy laden with nuts and berries.

"The nuts are sure to be all right; I expect the berries are too. I have certainly seen some like them in native markets, and I think it will be quite safe to risk it."

The rest of the day was spent in picking nuts and eating them. Then they sat down and waited for the arrival of their friend. He came two hours after nightfall with a wallet stored with provisions, and told them that he had regained the village unobserved. The attack had been repulsed, but with severe loss to the defenders as well as the assailants; two of their guards had been among the killed. The others had made a great clamour over the escape of the prisoners, and had made a close search throughout the village and immediately round it, for they were convinced that their captives had not had the strength to go any distance. He thought, however, that although they had professed the greatest indignation, and had offered many threats as to the vengeance that Government would take upon the village, one of whose inhabitants, at least, must have aided in the evasion of the prisoners, they would not trouble themselves any further in the matter. They had already reaped a rich harvest from the exhibition, and would divide among themselves the share of their late comrades; nor was it at all improbable that if they were to report the matter to the authorities they would themselves get into serious trouble for not having handed over the prisoners immediately after their capture.

For a fortnight the pilot nursed and fed the two midshipmen. He had already provided them with native clothes, so that if by chance any villagers should catch sight of them they would not recognize them as the escaped white men. At the end of that time both the lads had almost recovered from the effects of their sufferings. Jack, indeed, had picked up from the first, but Percy for some days continued so weak and ill that Jack had feared that he was going to have an attack of fever of some kind. His companion's cheery and hopeful chat did as much good for Percy as the nourishing food with which their friend supplied them, and at the end of the fortnight he declared that he felt sufficiently strong to attempt to make his way down to the coast.

The pilot acted as their guide. When they inquired about his wife, he told them carelessly that she would remain with her kinsfolk, and would travel on to Canton and join him there when she found an opportunity. The journey was accomplished at night, by very short stages at first, but by increasing distances as Percy gained strength. During the daytime the lads lay hid in woods or jungles, while their companion went into the village and purchased food. They struck the river many miles above Canton, and the pilot, going down first to a village on its banks, bargained for a boat to take him and two women down to the city.

The lads went on board at night and took their places in the little cabin formed of bamboos and covered with mats in the stern of the boat, and remained thus sheltered not only from the view of people in boats passing up or down the stream, but from the eyes of their own boatmen.

After two days' journey down the river without incident, they arrived off Canton, where the British fleet was still lying while negotiations for peace were being carried on with the authorities at Pekin. Peeping out between the mats, the lads caught sight of the English warships, and, knowing that there was now no danger, they dashed out of the cabin, to the surprise of the native boatmen, and shouted and waved their arms to the distant ships.

In ten minutes they were alongside the Perseus, when they were hailed as if restored from the dead. The pilot was very handsomely rewarded by the English authorities for his kindness to the prisoners, and was highly satisfied with the result of his proceedings, which more than doubled the little capital with which he had retired from business. Jack Fothergill and Percy Adcock declare that they have never since eaten chicken without thinking of their Christmas fare on the morning of their escape from the hands of the Chinese pirates.

www.ingramcontent.com/pod-product-compliance
Lightning Source LLC
Chambersburg PA
CBHW030416310726
48979CB00002B/441

* 9 7 9 8 8 8 0 9 0 0 0 9 1 *